D0455303

# I HATE BIRTHDAYS

## by The Old Man

Medium

I HATE BIRTHDAYS, I HATE SPRING. I HATE AL-MOST EV'-RY-THING.

I CAN BE NAS-TY, MEAN AND GRUMPY. I LIKE TO SLEEP ON A BED THAT'S LUMPY.

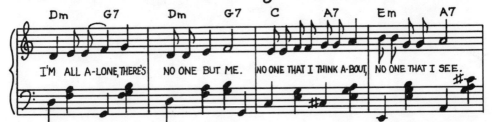

I'M ALL A-LONE, THERE'S NO ONE BUT ME. NO ONE THAT I THINK A-BOUT, NO ONE THAT I SEE.

NO ONE TO ASK ME, "HOW WAS YOUR DAY?" I'M ALL A-LONE AND I LIKE IT THAT WAY!

A Parents Magazine
READ ALOUD AND EASY READING PROGRAM® Original

Distributed in Canada by Clarke, Irwin & Co., Ltd.
Toronto, Canada

# The Old Man
## and the
# Afternoon Cat

by Michaela Muntean
pictures by Bari Weissman
music by Duncan Morrison

Parents Magazine Press • New York

To my sisters and brothers—M.M.


To Ron, Cynthia,
and their new baby—B.W.

Library of Congress Cataloging in Publication Data
Muntean, Michaela. The old man and the afternoon cat.
SUMMARY: An orange and white striped cat
causes a notorious grump to change his ways.
[1. Cats—Fiction.] I. Weissman, Bari, ill.
II. Title.
PZ7.M9290     [E]     81-11047
ISBN 0-8193-1071-9     AACR2
ISBN 0-8193-1072-7 (lib. bdg.)

Copyright © 1982 by Michaela Muntean.
Illustrations copyright © 1982 by Bari Weissman.
Music copyright © 1982 by Duncan Morrison.
All rights reserved.
Printed in the United States of America.
10   9   8   7   6   5   4   3   2   1

Every morning, the old man woke up
just as the sunlight began
peeking through his window.

He heard the birds singing.
He felt the gentle breezes blowing.
What a lovely way to start the day!

"Blech!" said the old man
as he sat up in bed.
He hurried to put on
his sunglasses and earmuffs.
"I hate sunlight and gentle breezes.
But most of all, I hate the sound
of birds singing."

Then the old man made his
favorite breakfast of burnt toast,
extra-hard boiled eggs and a big glass
of yucca berry juice to wash it all down.

"Harump," he said, when he finished.
"Now it is time for my grumbling exercises."

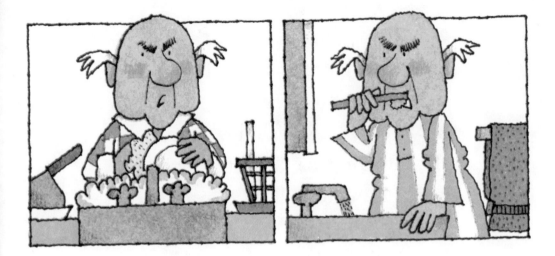

He grumbled as he washed the dishes.
He grumbled as he brushed his teeth.

He grumbled as he put on his
itchiest pair of itchy underwear.

Now it may seem to you that
there was nothing the old man liked.
But that is not true.
He liked to sing grumpy songs.
His favorite was, "I Hate Birthdays,"
which he wrote all by himself.

Here is how it goes in case
you are in a very grumpy mood
and would like to sing along:

# I HATE BIRTHDAYS

## by The Old Man

I hate birthdays, I hate spring.
I hate almost everything.
I can be nasty, mean and grumpy.
I like to sleep on a bed that's lumpy.
I'm all alone, there's no one but me.
No one that I think about,
no one that I see.
No one to ask me, "How was your day?"
I'm all alone and I like it that way!

After singing his song,
the old man was ready for his
outdoor grumbling exercises.
His neighbors were used
to his grumbling.
They just smiled and said, "Good day."
"Harump," the old man answered and
grumbled all the way to the park.

At the park, the old man sat far away
from everyone else to read his newspaper.
Then, he sat very quietly and waited.

Now, if you were sitting and waiting
as quietly as the old man,
you would hear it ...
a soft *pat-pat-pat,*
followed by a gentle crunch of leaves.

And if you were sitting
very, *very* quietly,
without a sneeze, or a cough,
or a rustle of a paper,
you would hear a soft and tiny
purring sound.

"Ah," said the old man.
"So you are back again."

And with that, up jumped
an orange and white striped cat.

Cats can take a long time
to get comfortable sometimes,
so the old man waited quietly
until the cat had snuggled just right.

Then the old man's chin dropped to
his chest and he began to snore.
And all afternoon they sat together,
the old man and the cat,
taking their afternoon nap.

When the cat woke up and stretched,
the old man woke up and stretched too.

Then they both went wherever it was
they had to go until the next afternoon.

But one day something strange happened.
The old man waited as quietly as usual.
He waited until all the mothers
took their babies home.

He waited until the man who sells
hot dogs and popcorn went home.

He waited until the sun went down
and the lights of the town
winked on in the darkness.
Finally, the old man went home.

The next day, the same thing happened.
"I wonder," said the old man,
"what has happened to my afternoon cat."
Then the old man began to worry.
He worried so hard that
he completely forgot about grumbling.

Finally, the old man knew what to do.
He drew a picture of the afternoon cat.
This is what it looked like:

The old man showed his picture
to everyone in the neighborhood.
"That's my morning cat!" said the grocer.
"I give him a fish tail every morning,
but I haven't seen him for days."

"Hmmm," said the baker.
"I can't be sure without my glasses,
but I think that's my lunch cat.
I give him a saucer of milk every day
at noon, but he's been gone for two days."

The school children knew him too.
"That's our after-school cat!" they cried.
"We give him pieces of our leftover lunch."

"My, my," said his neighbor, Mrs. McHatty.
"That's my evening cat.
I give him a cup of warm milk every night,
but I haven't seen him lately.
I hope nothing is wrong."

"If he's a stray," said the policeman,
"he was probably taken to The Cat Home."

The old man ran there as fast as he could.

Sure enough, there was the orange and white
striped cat, who purred a soft and tiny purr
when he saw the old man.

The woman in charge gave the cat
to the old man.
"You will need a tag for him," she said.
So the old man waited patiently
while the woman made the tag.

It said:

This is not a
stray cat.
He belongs to the
old man
and the old man
belongs to
him.

And with that, the old man and the cat went home.

Now every morning, the old man
and his cat visit the grocer.
She gives the cat a fish tail while
she and the old man have a cup of tea.

At noon, they visit the baker.
The old man and the baker share
a strawberry tart while the cat
has his saucer of milk.

Every day after school, the children
share their leftover lunches with the cat
and toss a ball with the old man.

And in the evenings, the old man chats
with his neighbor, Mrs. McHatty, while
the cat laps up his cup of warm milk.

The old man is so happy that he has
almost stopped grumbling completely.
Now he only grumbles
if he runs out of his favorite cereal,
or he can't find his socks,
or if it rains on the day
he wanted to go to the zoo.
But everyone grumbles about
those kinds of things sometimes,
because they're grumbly things.

Why, the old man even wrote a new song.
Here is how it goes, in case you
are in a very happy mood and
would like to sing along:

# I LIKE BIRTHDAYS

### by The Old Man

*I like birthdays, I like spring.*
*I like almost everything.*
*I like to smile and laugh and giggle.*
*I like to dance and hop and wiggle.*
*There's so many people*
*and places to see.*
*We are very busy, my cat and me.*
*We talk and visit and chat all day.*
*My afternoon cat and I like it that way!*

*(Meow)*

## About the Author

Not long ago, a friend who could no longer keep her cat asked MICHAELA MUNTEAN to care for it. Ms. Muntean always loved cats, and so she was happy to take Gaspar. Gaspar is now very much at home with Ms. Muntean: waking her in the morning, curling up in her lap, spending lazy afternoons lying in the sun. "You can't ever really *own* a cat," Ms. Muntean says. "But it's a lot of fun when one comes to live with you."

Michaela Muntean is the author of many well-loved children's books, including THE VERY BUMPY BUS RIDE and A GARDEN FOR MISS MOUSE for Parents.

Ms. Muntean, and Gaspar, live in New York City.

## About the Artist

BARI WEISSMAN has a black and white cat named Oboe. Ms. Weissman says that most of the time Oboe just sleeps. But when he isn't sleeping, he's grumbling. "He's the grumbly one in our household," she explains. He grumbles for his food, he grumbles to be let outside, he grumbles for a hug. "But when he gets what he wants," Ms. Weissman says, "he stops grumbling and purrs."

Bari Weissman's bright and bold illustrations have enlivened many picture books, including GOLLY GUMP SWALLOWED A FLY for Parents.

Ms. Weissman lives with her husband, and Oboe, in Brighton, Massachusetts.

# I LIKE BIRTHDAYS

## by The Old Man